Feathers

A Jewish Tale from Eastern Europe

Retold by Heather Forest

Illustrated by Marcia Cutchin

AUGUST HOUSE
LittleFolk

LITTLE ROCK

For my father and mother
-H.F.
And for my mom and dad, Trudy and Jim Maxwell
-M.C.

Text copyright © 2005 by Heather Forest.
Illustrations copyright © 2005 by Marcia Cutchin.

Published 2005 by August House LittleFolk,
P.O. Box 3223, Little Rock, Arkansas 72203
501-372-5450
http://www.augusthouse.com

Book design by Harvill Ross Studio Ltd.
Manufactured in Korea
10 9 8 7 6 5 4 3 2 1 HC

LIBRARY OF CONGRESS CATALOGING-IN-PUBLICATION DATA
Forest, Heather
Feathers : a Jewish tale from Eastern Europe / retold by Heather Forest ; illustrated by Marcia Cutchin.
p. cm.
Summary: A wise rabbi uses a pillow full of feathers to teach a gossipy villager a lesson.
ISBN 0-87483-755-3.
[1. Jews—Folklore 2. Folklore—Europe, Eastern.] I. Cutchin, Marcia, 1958– ill. II. Title.
PZ8.1.F76Fea 2005
398.2'089'924—dc22
[E]   2005041115

The paper used in this publication meets the minimum requirements of the American National Standards for Information Sciences
Permanence of Paper for Printed Library Materials, ANSI.48–1984.

Author's Note
This Jewish tale, attributed to Rabbi Levi Yitzhak of Berdichev, an 18th century Eastern European Hasidic rabbi, has traveled far.
It has been retold again and again by teachers and storytellers over the centuries to illustrate the power of the spoken word.
Words can teach, heal, and inspire. When misused, careless words can be a cruel weapon, as anyone who has ever been the victim of a rumor knows.

Feathers

Words, like feathers fly
in the wind, in the wind.
Reaching far and wide,
in the wind, in the wind.
Careless words, tossed about,
cannot again be swallowed up.
Tongues like swords can cut the heart.
Words fly out.
The rumors start . . .

Once, in a village not far away,

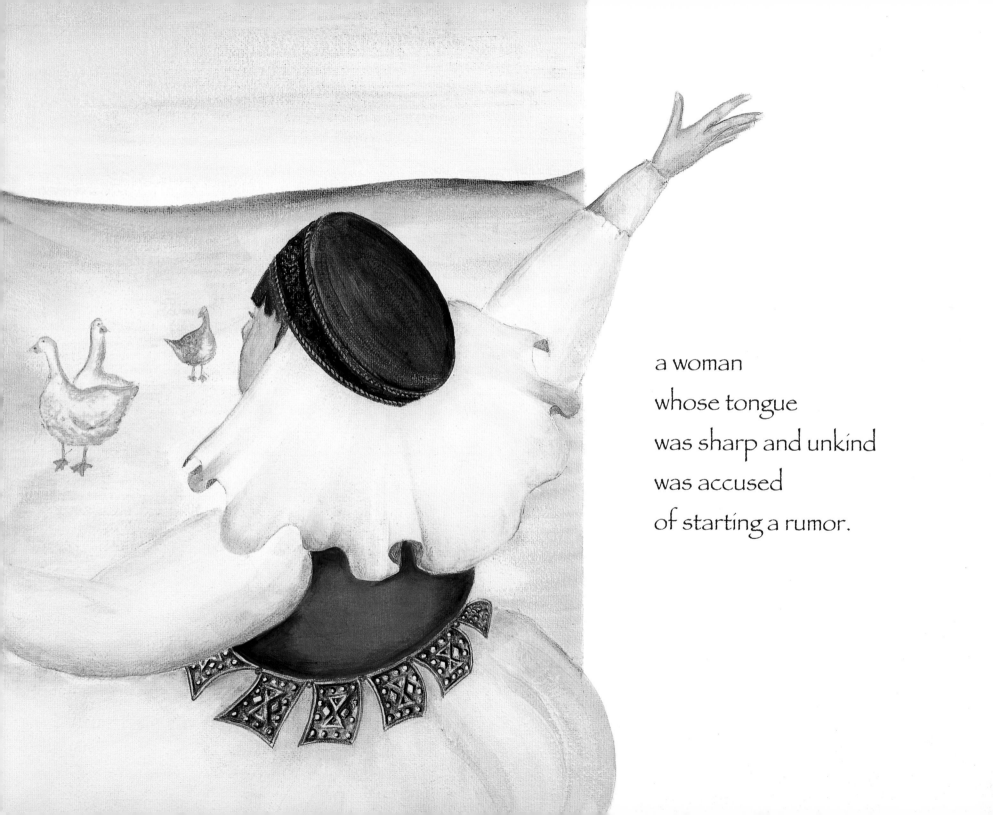

a woman
whose tongue
was sharp and unkind
was accused
of starting a rumor.

She was brought before
the village rabbi, protesting,
"What I said was in jest,
just humor.
My words were carried
forth by others.
I am not to blame."

But the victim cried
for justice saying,
"You have soiled
my own good name."

"I can make amends," said the woman accused.

"I will take back my words

and assume
I'm excused."

The rabbi listened
to what she said
and sadly thought
as he shook his head,
"This woman does not
understand her crime.
She shall do it again
and again in time."

So he said to the woman accused,

"Your careless words cannot be excused until . . .

you take my feather pillow to the market square.

Cut it open and let
the feathers fly through the air.

When this task is done,
bring back the feathers,
every one."

The woman reluctantly agreed.
She thought,
"The wise old rabbi's gone mad indeed!"

But to humor him,
she took his pillow to the village square.
She cut it open . . .

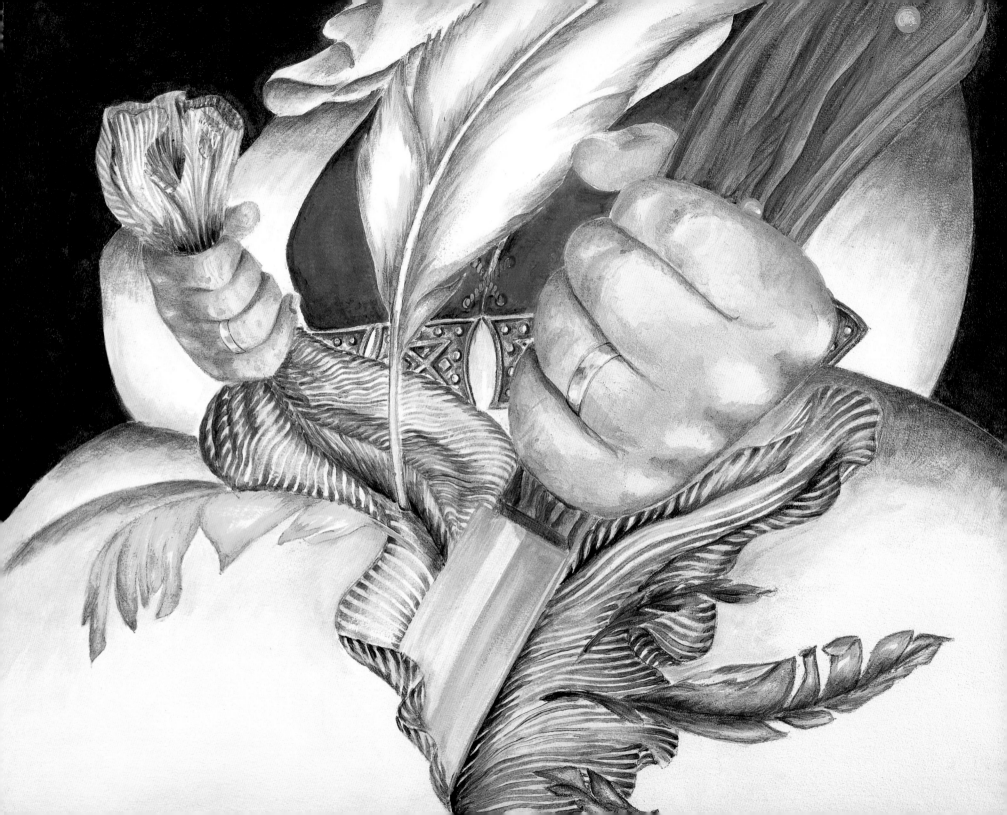

and feathers filled the air.

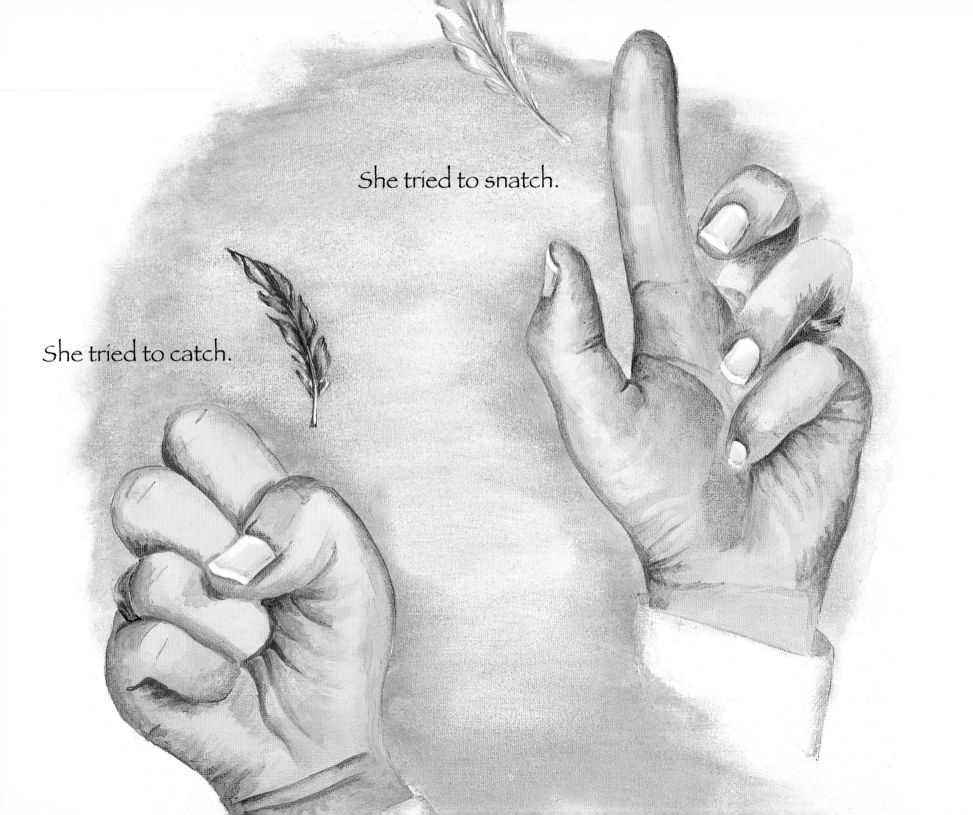

She tried to snatch.

She tried to catch.

She tried to collect each one.

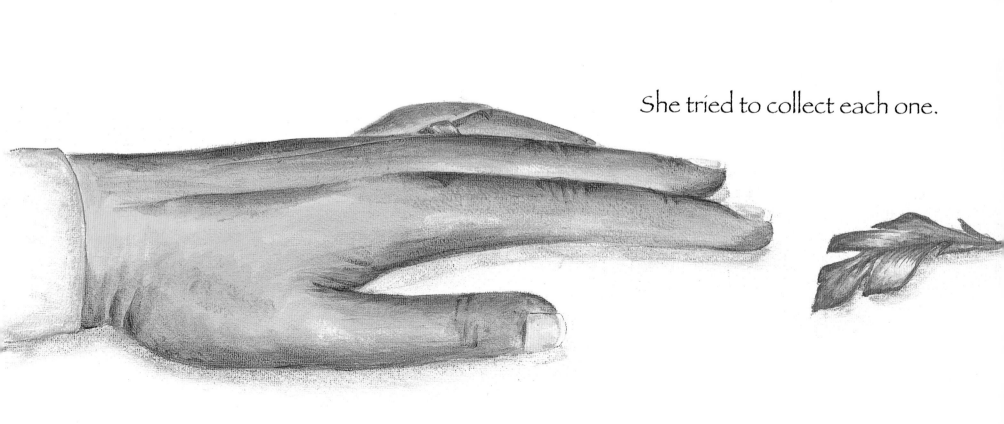

But weary with effort,
she quickly discovered
the task could not be done.

She returned with very few of the feathers in hand.
"I cannot bring them back. They have scattered over the land!"

"I suppose," she sighed
as she lowered her head,
"They are like the words
I can't take back,

from the rumor I spread."

Cruel words like feathers fly.
Cruel words reach far and wide.
They leave the mouth a bitter rind.

May all your words,
my friends, be kind.